Zoom Squirrel

Zing Squirrel

Flappy Squirrel

Norman

Quiz Squirrel

Research Rodent

Wink Squirrel

Look!
A **book**!

Klink Squirrel

This is a **big book!**

It is **full** of . . .

BIG
FUN!

HYPERION BOOKS FOR CHILDREN / *NEW YORK*
AN IMPRINT OF DISNEY BOOK GROUP

To Cher!

Hi! I'm **Zip Squirrel**! There is so much to read in this book!

So, let's **zip to it**, Squirrel pals! It's the **table of contents**!

TABLE OF CONTENTS

Look for the **EMOTE-ACORNS** in this story. They pop up when the Squirrels have **BIG** feelings!

CONFUSED

SURPRISED

SAD

DETERMINED

SCARED

HAPPY

FUNNY

The BIG Story!

I LOST MY TOOTH!

Th!

By **Mo Willems**

I lost my tooth, **Th-ap** Squirrel.

"**Zap**" Squirrel.

?

You should not let a tooth go **loose**, Zoom Squirrel.

Teeth have no **sense of direction**.

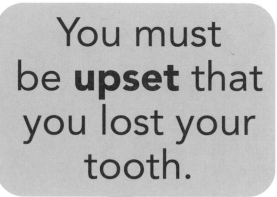

You must be **upset** that you lost your tooth.

It is **okay**!

Do **not** worry!

Because...

14

WE WILL FIND YOUR TOOTH!

We will look **near!**

We will look **far!**

Um...

We will **ask** every Squirrel!

We will **describe** the tooth!

How?

We do **not** know what the tooth looks like!

18

A BABY

Poor **baby!**

All **alone!**

It is **sooooooo** sad!

It must be **hungry!**

Boo-hoo!

25

SQUIRRELS AWAY!

Maybe it fell
out while I was
sleeping....

I will check **under my pillow!**

Bad news, Zoom Squirrel. We did **not** find the baby tooth.

Zoom Squirrel?

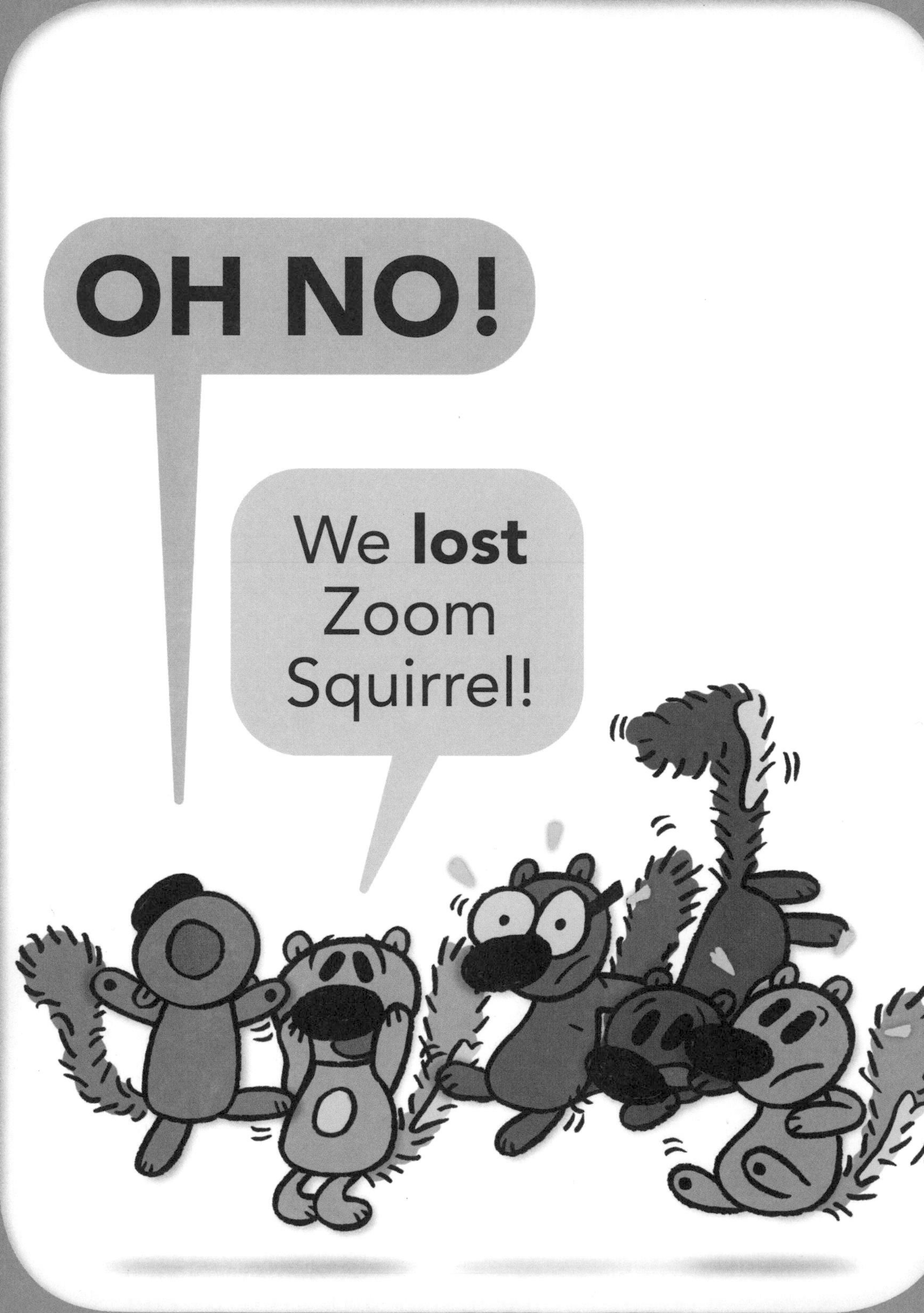
OH NO!
We **lost** Zoom Squirrel!

And I
thought this was
going to be
a **happy** story.

SQUIRRELS!

Look!

Zoom Squirrel is **back**!

Hi, guy-**th**!

With—

THE BABY TOOTH!

It **could** mean that Zoom Squirrel **found** the tooth…

Or it could mean…

THE TOOTH FOUND

ZOOM SQUIRREL!!!

Sweetie!

I will get the **baby buggy**!

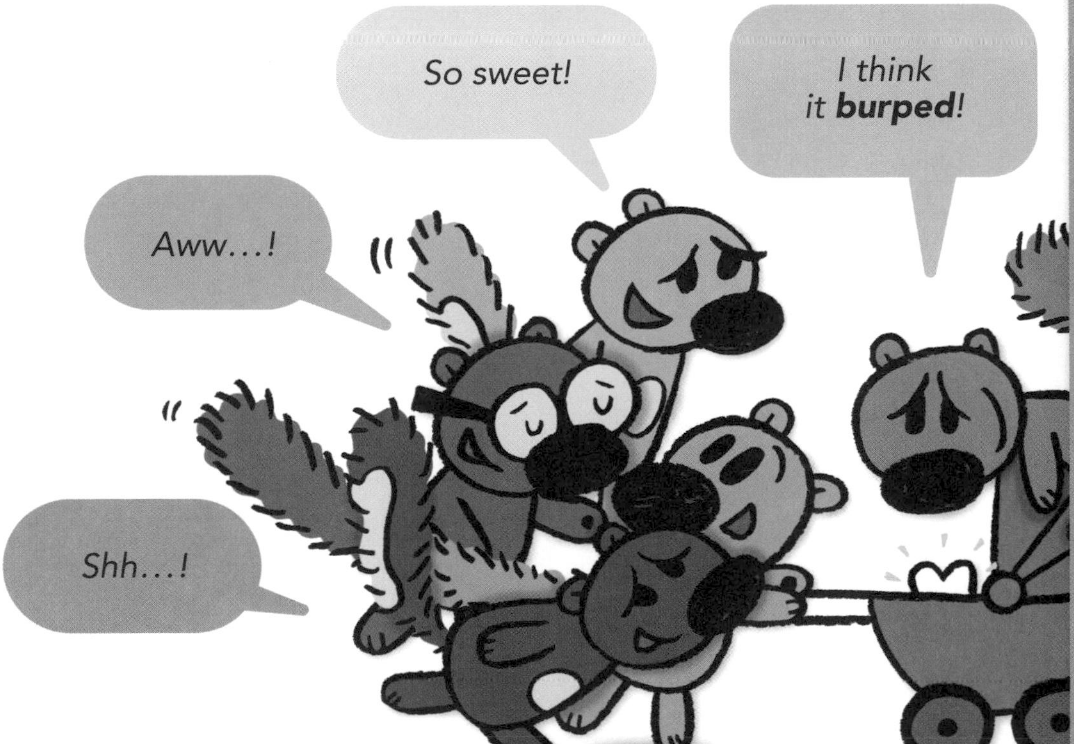
So sweet!
I think
it **burped**!
Aww…!
Shh…!

I **learned** something today.

Wiggle
Wiggle
Wiggle

Pluck!

A bunch of **"TOOTHS"**!

65

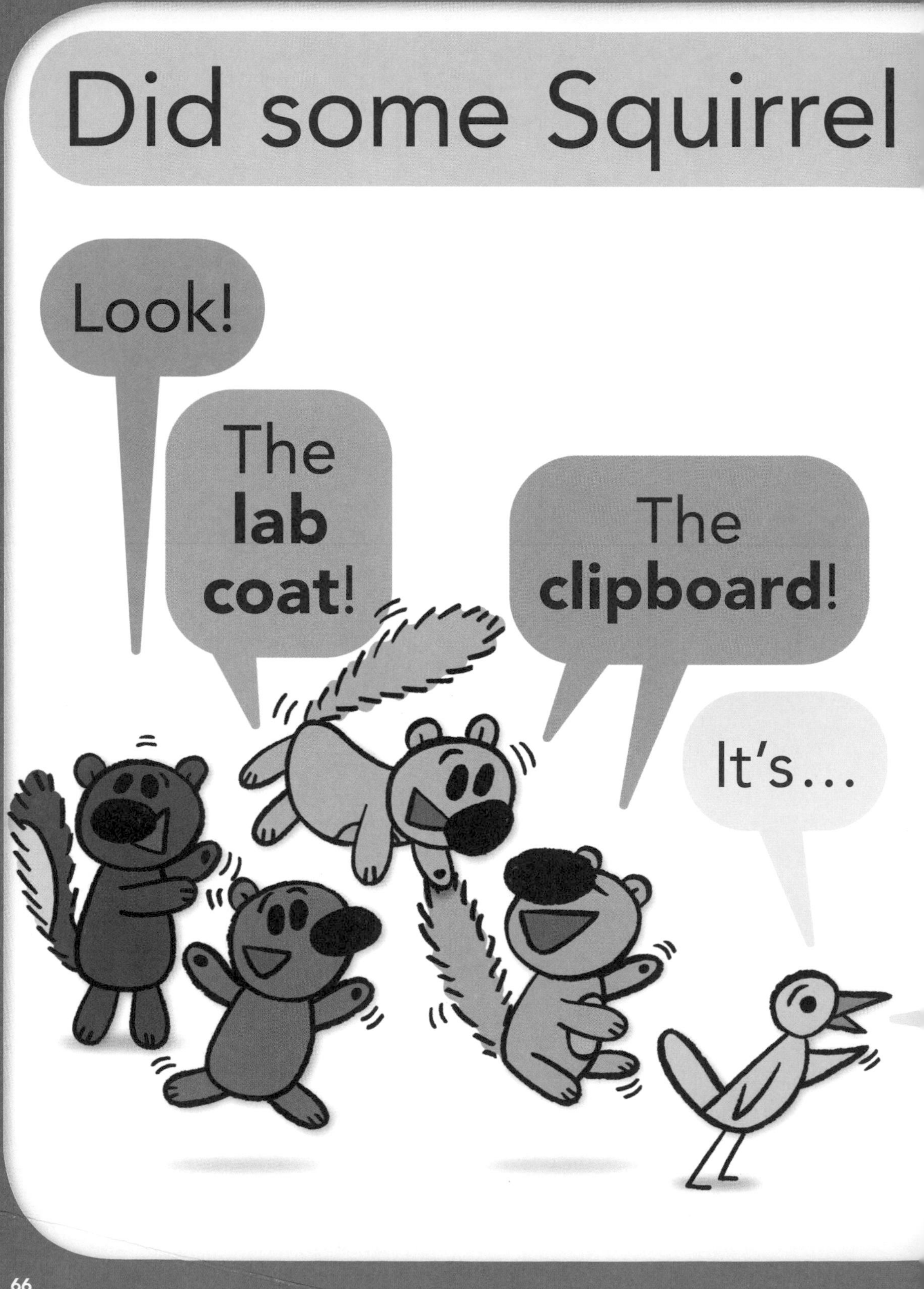
Did some Squirrel
Look!
The **lab coat**!
The **clipboard**!
It's...

THE SQUIRRELLY TOOTH TRUTH

Unlike in Zoom Squirrel's **BIG STORY**, squirrels do **NOT** lose their front teeth!

Squirrels **DO** lose their back baby teeth. They grow new ones just like you do.

Squirrels use their front teeth for opening food, such as nuts and fruit.

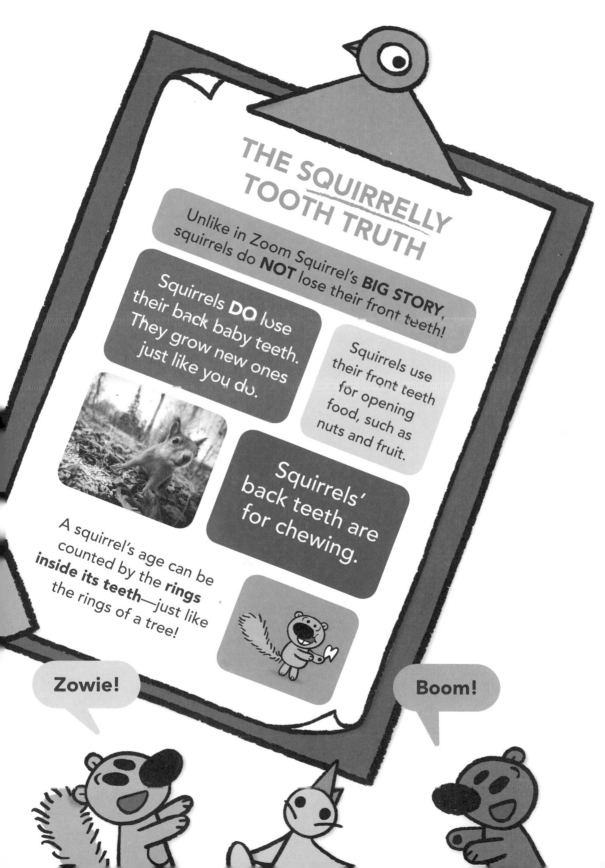

Squirrels' back teeth are for chewing.

A squirrel's age can be counted by the **rings** **inside its teeth**—just like the rings of a tree!

Zowie!

Boom!

HOORAY FOR RESEARCH RODENT!

Research **rocks**— that's a **theory!**

A **CHOO-CHOO** TRAIN!

Har!

Hee!

Ha!

Hee!

Ha!

Har!

Har!

Hee!

Ha!

Har!

Ha!

Har!

Hee!

A joke with **bite**!

It was **hard to swallow**!

IT'S

FUR REAL!

WITH QUIZ SQUIRREL

I'm **Quiz Squirrel** and this **quiz** is my **biz**!

Think about it.
Who has **ONLY** one set
of **BABY TEETH?**

A **bear**?
A **shark**?
A **houseplant**?

Do **you** know
the answer?
Say it **out loud**
(and say **why**).

Then, **turn
the page**!

It's
THE BEAR!

THE WILD TOOTH

Brown bears, black bears, polar bears—even panda bears—have **only** one set of baby teeth that they lose and replace. A grown-up bear has up to 42 teeth.

Sharks can grow and lose **thousands** of teeth in a lifetime.

Plants **do not** have teeth. That is okay— neither do birds! But snakes **do** have teeth. Some spiders, snails, and slugs have teeth, too.

I **do not** have teeth?

But you **do** have friends, Flappy Squirrel!

Learn more **WILD FACTS** at UnlimitedSquirrels.com!

This is **Quiz Squirrel** saying:

*There's always something more to **learn**—when you have a page to **turn**!*

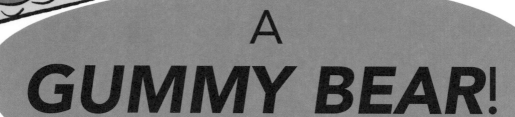

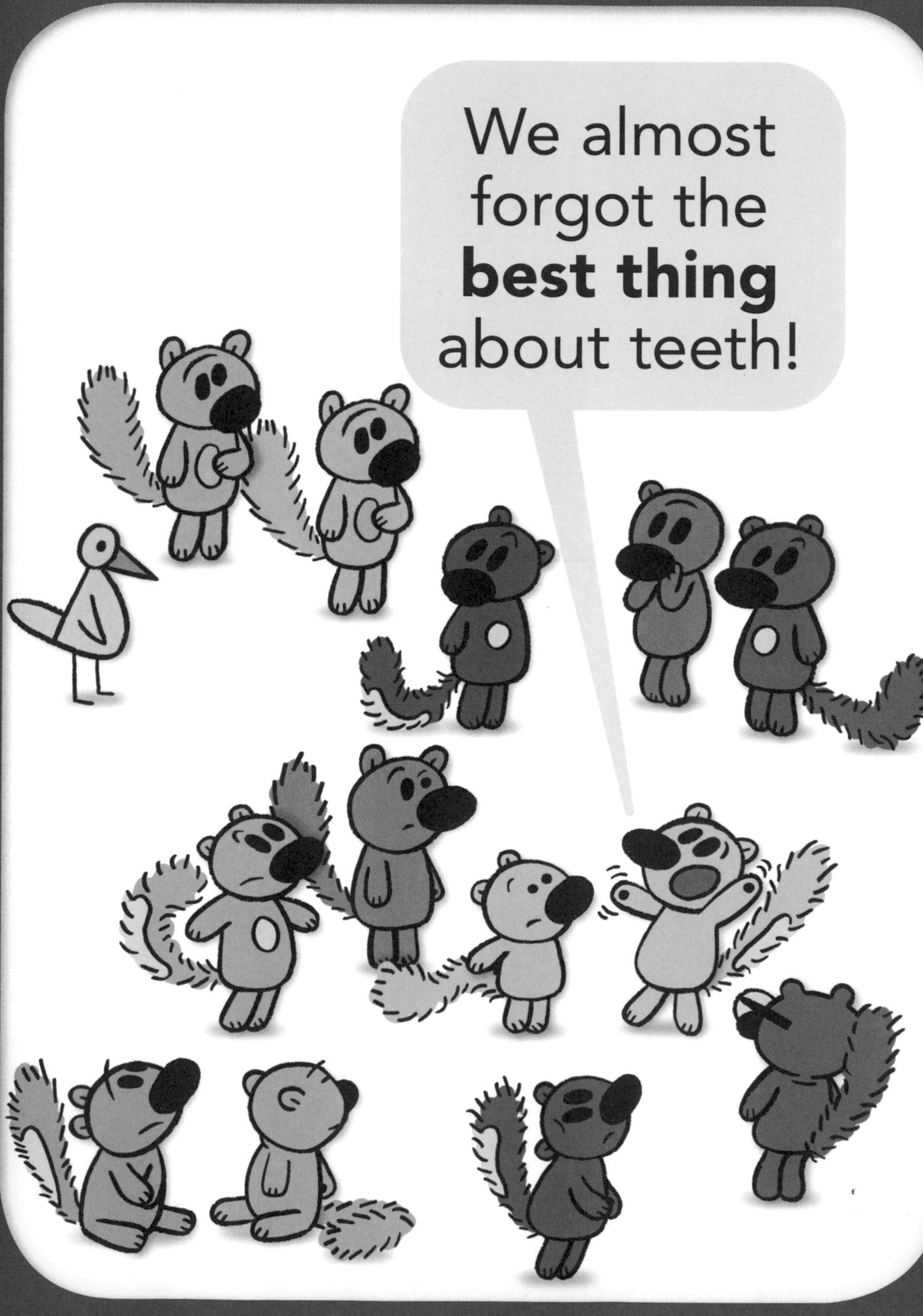
We almost forgot the **best thing** about teeth!

Photos © Shutterstock: Toy Teeth: Hurst Photo; Squirrel: Everst; Brown Bear: Image Source Trading Ltd; Great White Shark: Jim Agronick; Houseplant: Horiyan

Printed in Malaysia
Reinforced binding

First Edition, October 2018
10 9 8 7 6 5 4 3 2 1
FAC-029191-18187

Library of Congress Cataloging-in-Publication Data

Names: Willems, Mo, author, illustrator.
Title: I lost my tooth! / by Mo Willems.
Description: First edition. • New York : Hyperion Books For Children, 2018.
 Series: Unlimited squirrels ; [1] • Summary: Friends search for Zoom
 Squirrel's missing baby tooth. Includes "acorn-y jokes" and "cool facts."
Identifiers: LCCN 2018000644 • ISBN 9781368024570 (paper over board)
Subjects: • CYAC: Teeth—Fiction. • Squirrels—Fiction. • Humorous stories.
Classification: LCC PZ7.W65535 Iaj 2018 • DDC [E]—dc23
LC record available at https://lccn.loc.gov/2018000644

Visit www.hyperionbooksforchildren.com and www.pigeonpresents.com

A BIG SQUIRRELLY THANK-YOU TO OUR EXPERTS!

Louise Emmons, Research Associate, Division of Mammals, Smithsonian Institution

Peter S. Ungar, author of *Evolution's Bite: A Story of Teeth, Diet and Human Origins* and *Teeth: A Very Short Introduction*, and director of the Environmental Dynamics Program at the University of Arkansas